Sink or Swim

Ghillian Potts

Illustrated by Jan Lewis

YOUNG CORGI

SINK OR SWIM
A YOUNG CORGI BOOK : 0 552 52753X

First published in Great Britain by Young Corgi Books

PRINTING HISTORY
Young Corgi edition published 1993
Reissued Young Corgi edition published 2002

1 3 5 7 9 10 8 6 4 2

Set in 16/20pt Bembo Schoolbook

Young Corgi Books are published by Transworld Publishers,
61–63 Uxbridge Road, London W5 5SA,
a division of The Random House Group Ltd,
in Australia by Random House Australia (Pty) Ltd,
20 Alfred Street, Milsons Point, Sydney, NSW 2061, Australia,
in New Zealand by Random House New Zealand Ltd,
18 Poland Road, Glenfield, Auckland 10, New Zealand
and in South Africa by Random House (Pty) Ltd,
Endulini, 5a Jubilee Road, Parktown 2193, South Africa

Printed and bound in Great Britain by
Cox & Wyman Ltd, Reading, Berkshire

SINK OR SWIM

Chapter One

William got up early that morning, because it was Tuesday.

First, he went to check on his mum. He wanted to be sure she was all right.

She was. Fast asleep and breathing steadily, just as she always was at six o'clock.

William was glad he'd learned to tell the time and Mum had given him the clock. It had a loud friendly tick, so William always knew it was working. It was an alarm clock but the alarm part was broken. That didn't matter to William. He always woke early.

Before he'd learned to tell the time, William had got up to check on his mum as soon as he woke. Often enough he'd woken her up, leaning against her to be sure she was breathing all right.

"William Waters," his mum would say, every time. "I do NOT want to be woken up at four in the morning!" (or whatever time it was). "I have to go to work and I need my sleep. Now you go right back to bed this minute and I don't want a peep out of you till seven o'clock."

And William would say, "But how do I know when it's seven o'clock?"

"Because that's when I come and say to you, 'Time to get up, William!' That's how," his mum used to say.

These days, William could look at his clock and say to himself, "Six o'clock. Not time yet."

And now he was bigger, he didn't need to lean on his mum to check she was breathing. He was tall enough to lean over without touching and not wake her.

So that's what he did, every morning. His mum laughed at him.

"I'm all right," she told him. "You don't need to worry about me. I'm always all right."

But William worried just the same.

Today, he got dressed as soon as he'd checked on his mum. Tuesday was

swimming day and he was worried
about his swimming things. Once, his
mum had forgotten to put his trunks
inside his towel and everyone had
laughed at him. He'd had to sit at the
side of the pool and watch, all through
the swimming lesson.

So now, every Tuesday, William got
up early. He checked on his mum and
got dressed. Then he fetched his special
swimming towel out of the airing
cupboard and his swimming trunks out
of the drawer under his bed, rolled the
trunks up in the towel and put them by
the front door, all ready.

Finally, he checked his mum again. This time she was awake.

"You're up early, William," she said. "Swimming day, is it?"

William nodded. He didn't talk much. His mum didn't mind. "William's a good listener," she said. "And I talk enough for two."

"Good listeners are few and far between," she told William. "Talkers are two-a-penny!"

So William didn't mind either.

Mum got up and made their breakfast. William watched the kettle in case it boiled over.

"We'll get an electric kettle one day," promised his mum. "The sort that turns itself off when it's boiled."

William watched the toast as well, to see that it didn't burn.

"It could catch fire and burn the house down!" he said.

"No chance," said his mum. "Cookers are meant to be hot. If the toast did catch fire, only the toast would burn. Nothing else."

William still watched it. Just in case.

When it was time for Mum to go to work, it was time for William to go to school.

He went with Mum to the bus stop. It was near his school.

"Will you be working late tonight?" he asked. He hated it when his mum got home late. He never knew what might have happened to her.

"Not today," said Mum. "Look, there's my bus. Give us a kiss and be good!" She hugged him and jumped on the bus.

William watched it out of sight. It didn't crash. But of course he couldn't

 watch it all the way to Mum's stop. It could crash anywhere.

William walked to school very carefully. If I hold my breath till the traffic lights change, she'll be all right, he promised himself.

He felt ready to burst but he held his breath until the green light changed to amber. Then he had to let it out.

I only said "change", he thought. I didn't say "change to red". It's all right. I'm sure it's all right.

Chapter Two

William was always early getting to school because Mum had to go to work long before school began. Usually he was first in the playground.

So he was surprised to see Big Mark zooming round the empty playground. He was being a motorcycle. William thought it might be a Honda.

Big Mark was the biggest boy in William's class. He was a banger. He banged around all the time, knocking the other children over. Once he  even knocked their teacher, Miss Gowan, over. But that was an accident.

It was very unusual for Big Mark to be there so early. Big Mark liked rushing round the playground before school started, banging into the other children while they waited for the bell to ring and again while they tried to line up to go in. But it was no fun unless there were plenty of people to bang into. So Mark usually came charging in at the gate about five minutes before the bell went.

Today, his mum's watch was fast and she had chased Mark out of the house half an hour early. So when Mark found the playground empty, with no-one to bang into, he was cross.

He kicked his bag with his swimming things and his pencil-case in it right over the spiked railings into the playground. Then he turned himself into a motorcycle, revved himself up, bounced once on his rear wheel and roared into the playground.

When he saw William coming, he zoomed straight at him. William jumped sideways and was a traffic policeman.

He held up one hand and waved Big Mark on with the other. He thought Big Mark might be a mad motorcycle that would run even a police-man down, but it was worth trying.

Big Mark stopped. He was riding his motorcycle now, not being it, so that he could talk to William. He honked his horn and made his engine roar and said, "You're a weed, William."

William decided to be a traffic light. He stood very stiff and said in a com-puter voice, "My. light. is. green. You. may. proceed."

So Big Mark zoomed away, banked round a turn by the rubbish bins and came back.

"You're a weedy weed," he said. "There's a flower called Sweet William, my mum says. So you must be a weed."

William thought that Big Mark was going to zoom at him and knock him down. He shut his eyes.

Nothing happened.

He opened his eyes. Big Mark was staring at him.

"Aren't you going to do anything?" he asked.

William thought.

"No," he said.

Big Mark made a ph-ttt noise. "You ARE a weed," he said.

He zoomed off to bang into some girls who had just come into the playground.

William stood and watched.

The girls screeched and one of them
swung her shoe-bag at Big Mark's
head. It missed.

Big Mark laughed. He was pleased
that the girls had screamed.

He wants me to scream, thought
William. Well, I won't.

Chapter Three

When William's class got to the swimming baths, the attendant said,

"Now, you lot, no pushing people in and no ducking other people! Or I shall make you come out of the water."

She said this every time and every
time someone got pushed in and several
people got ducked. But no-one ever said
who had done it, so the attendant never
did make anyone come out of the pool.

Often it was William who got
ducked. He didn't mind being pushed in.
He never shrieked the way all the others
did, so he wasn't pushed in much.

But he hated being ducked. He tried
always to keep
close to the side
of the pool, to
make it harder
for anyone to
come up behind
him. This was not
good for his swimming, of course. In
fact, no-one had ever seen William
swim properly.

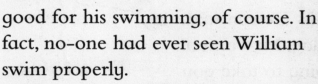

Miss Gowan, William's teacher, sometimes said, "Come on, William, let's see
what you can do!"

But William would just look at her
and wade or pull himself sideways
along the rail with his back to the side
of the pool.

Miss Gowan never nagged. She
sighed and said, "All right, William.
When you're ready, you'll swim."

Today, something different
happened.

Miss Gowan had a new
teacher with her. He was
large and bouncy and he
grinned all the time.

He made William think
of a big, friendly dog who
hopes you are taking
him for a walk.

Miss Gowan said,
"Today, Mr Timson
is going to take you
for swimming. He is a very good swimmer
himself, so you must all show him how
well you can do."

"You a student teacher, then, Sir?" asked Big Mark.

Mr Timson grinned his big, cheerful grin. "That's right," he said. "See my L-plates, did you?"

Everybody laughed. Big Mark laughed loudest.

Mr Timson wanted to know who couldn't swim yet.

Several people put up a hand.

"Who can swim a width?" asked Mr Timson.

More hands went up.

"Can anyone do a whole length?" Mr Timson grinned eagerly at them.

Big Mark and two others put up their hands. After a moment, so did William. Mr Timson did look so hopeful. He wanted them to be able to swim a length. William felt sorry for Mr Timson. And he knew he could do it, easily. Even though he never swam in the class.

Miss Gowan looked as if she was going to say something to Mr Timson. Then she shut her mouth again.

Mr Timson asked the people who couldn't swim to wait a little while. "I'll get back to you in a few minutes," he promised. "I just want to see how fast this lot can swim."

The people who could swim a width went first. They made a lot of noise, splashing and squealing and yelling "You put your foot on the bottom!", "No I didn't!" and things like that.

Carol Lamb won. She bounced up
and down screaming "Yayy!!" until Miss
Gowan told her to be quiet.

Miss Gowan looked as if she had a
headache, thought William. She often
had one after swimming lessons.
"Couldn't you scream a bit more
quietly?" she said sometimes. "My head
is splitting!"

Then it was the turn of the people
who said they could do a length.

"Now then, you four. Hop in the water
at the deep end," called Mr Timson.

William, Harriet and Kamlesh hopped. They hooked their feet under the rail and floated. "No, don't dive," called Mr Timson, sharply. "Stop!"

William twisted round to look up.

Big Mark dived in on top of him.

William went under.

The water rushed greenly into his eyes and nose and mouth. He fought it and fought it but the waves were too big for him and the current too strong. The harsh bitter taste of salt sea water filled his throat as he choked and struggled and then, just like before, the blackness came down.

Chapter Four

Miss Gowan was crying. "I knew I should have warned you!" she said in a funny choking voice. "Oh, I could kill that Mark Kimber! Now William may never get his nerve back."

William tried to sit up. He was all wrapped up in a big towel and Miss Gowan had her arms round him. She let go of him and wiped her eyes quickly on a corner of the towel.

"Well, you did give us a fright, William!" she said in a bright voice.

William looked round. He was in a
small room lined with green painted
lockers. Mr Timson stood in the door-
way. His grin was gone. He looked like
a retriever that has lost the stick you
threw him.

"Where'd the sea go?" asked William.
The taste in his mouth was the taste of
swimming bath chemicals, not bitter
salt.

Then he remembered.

He stood up. Miss Gowan stood up, too. "I'll ring your mum at work, as soon as we get back to school," she said. "She can take the day off and look after you. You've had a nasty shock, William. I think you'd be better off at home."

William was worried. "You mustn't!" he said. "Mum could get the sack if she's off work! I'm OK, really I am."

Mr Timson cleared his throat. "I guess I'll have to fill in an accident form," he said. He sounded miserable.

Miss Gowan said, "You get dressed, William, and we'll see how you feel. Here's your things."

She took Mr Timson outside and shut the door.

William felt a bit funny. His hands seemed as if they were shaking but, when he looked at them, they weren't. And his legs kept trying to bend. But he told himself firmly that he was quite all right and by the time he'd pulled his clothes on, it was almost true.

Everyone was very quiet going back to school. The girls whispered together and no-one talked to Big Mark. He came and sat next to William in the school bus.

"Hey, it was an accident!" he said. "I never meant to, like, drown you!"

William tried to think of something to say. "No," he said at last. "No, I didn't think you did."

He didn't think it was quite an accident, either. Big Mark had meant to land too close to him and scare him.

He didn't say anything else and Big Mark said nothing more to him. Instead, he twisted round and whistled until Miss Gowan said, "Shut up, Mark!" in a voice that sounded so unlike her that everyone stared at her.

William was not sent home. The school nurse came and looked at him and took his temperature and asked if he wanted to lie down in the sickroom. But William said, "No, thank you," in his politest voice and she smiled and sent him back to his classroom.

When he got home after school, Mum was already there. Miss Gowan had rung her at work, after all, and she had come home early.

33

William was angry. He didn't like
grown-ups doing things over his head.
They always said it was for his own
good but to William it felt like being
interfering. Suppose Mum got into
trouble for coming away from work
early?

He didn't say anything but his mum
knew.

"It's all right, darling," she said. "Miss
Gowan was worried about you, that's
all. And my boss
really didn't
mind me leaving
a few minutes
early. He was
very nice about
it. And I've
bought some of
that raspberry ice
cream you like,
for tea."

"Oh," said William. "Thanks, Mum."

He didn't say anything about Big Mark or the swimming baths and his mum didn't ask. They ate the ice cream and watched some telly and William went to bed early because he was tired.

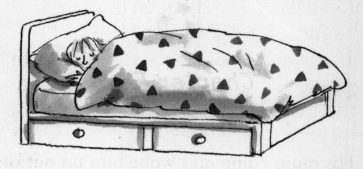

But that night he had the bad dream again.

Chapter Five

His mum came and woke him up out of the dream, just as he was sinking for the last time. She brought him a drink of hot milk and honey and told him stories until he went to sleep again.

In the morning, they both woke late.

"I'll write you a note for Miss Gowan," said Mum, cheerfully. "No need to worry."

"But what about you? Your boss will be angry with you," said William. He was too worried to eat his breakfast.

"Oh, you'll have to write me a note!" said Mum, laughing.

And William did.

Please don't be cross. Mum is late because I woke her up in the night. I am very sorry,
love,
William.

he wrote.

He gave Mum's note to Miss Gowan when he got to school. It was nearly playtime, he was so late. Miss Gowan asked him to help her sort out the coloured crayons till the bell rang.

Big Mark banged into William when they went out to play. William wanted to bang him back. But he didn't. He picked himself up and walked right across the playground, straight through everybody's games, and stood staring out through the railings at the road.

The shops on the other side of the road were dull, but he went on looking at them for several minutes.

Then Harriet came up behind him and said, "I'm going to get that Mark!"

She sounded furious. William turned
to look at her. She looked furious, too.
There was blood oozing from her
grazed knee. She
stopped sucking
the side of her
hand for a
moment and
said, "I'll
'Screw his
neck and drink
his blood!'" She
sounded ghoulish.

"'And leave his body lying!'" finished
William.

"'Around the rick, around the rick,
And there I met my Uncle Dick,
I screwed his neck and sucked his
blood…'"

"'And left the body lying!'" they
chanted together.

Harriet laughed and William laughed
too. He felt more cheerful.

"We could get him," he said, thinking about it. "We could make him sorry."

Harriet gave up trying to lick the blood off her knee and spat on her hanky instead. "How?" she said.

William thought some more.

"Well," he said, "Big Mark likes the people he bangs into and knocks over to scream and carry on, doesn't he?"

"Go on," said Harriet. She beckoned to her best friend Rachel. Rachel came over and listened.

"If we could get everyone to pretend not to notice Big Mark, even when he bangs into them," said William, "he'd really hate that, wouldn't he?"

"You'd never get everyone to agree," said Rachel. She whistled through her fingers and some more girls came over. One or two boys came as well.

William said nothing. Perhaps it wasn't a good idea after all. Even if it worked, maybe Big Mark wouldn't care. Maybe, thought William, worried, he'd get worse.

"It's a marvellous idea!" said Harriet. "Now listen, you lot," she told the small crowd gathered around them. "William's got this great idea. We're fed up of Big Mark bashing into us all the time and we're going to stop him. But you'll all

have to help. Me and William and
Rachel can't do it on our own."

"What do we have to do?" asked Pat.
His ginger hair bristled and his eyes
sparkled. "Bash him back?"

"NO!" Harriet glared at him. "No,
what you all have to do is NOTHING!"

"Huh?" said everyone.

"You explain to them, William," said
Rachel. "Shut up and listen, the lot of
you! We don't want Big Mark to know!"

William could feel himself going red.
He whispered to Harriet, "You tell them!"

Harriet poked him in the ribs so that he couldn't help giggling.

"It's your idea, dafty," she said kindly. "You get an idea, you get to tell about it, OK?"

So William explained. He stared at the ground and hurried to get it over.

"If he bangs into you, pretend it hasn't happened," he said.

"What? Can't hear you!" called Rav.

William tried to speak louder. "Make as if you haven't noticed him," he said. "Don't squeak or cry and DON'T hit back. He'll hate it. You'll see. He'll be really miserable. Only it's got to be all of us."

William hadn't said so much all at once since he started school. All the others listened, surprised.

"Umm," said Pat, "I'd still like to bash him back. But I'll give it a go."

Georgina said, "Me, too. You'll help, won't you, Wayne?"

Wayne had huge scabs on his skinny knees. Big Mark knocked him over a lot. "I'm on," he said.

"So's me and Harriet," said Rachel. "What about the rest of you?"

They all agreed.

"Now we get hold of all the other kids," said Harriet. "Everyone small enough for Mark to bang into. Split up, and get it organized. In twos,

that'll be best. And DON'T let Big
Mark know!"

William watched in amazement as
his idea spread through the playground.

Chapter Six

That evening, Mum brought back a
note from her boss for William.
   It said:

Grafton Enterprises PLC,
61 Ford Street

Dear William,
   Thank you for your letter. Please don't
worry. I am not cross at all. Your mum is
such a good worker that I don't mind if she
has a little time off.
   Yours sincerely, Geo. F. Lees.

"What's Geo?" asked William.

"Short for George," said Mum.

"Oh," said William. He put the letter away in the drawer under his bed. It was the first letter he'd ever had with a real printed address at the top.

Now he knew where Mum worked. He hadn't known before. He had been there, but he'd never noticed the road or the number of the office. He liked knowing. It made Mum's work seem more real. And he could find her if he ever needed to.

He took the safe feeling to school with him on Thursday.

He found Harriet, Rachel and Kamlesh in the playground. They had come early specially, to organize the girls.

Rachel waited by the gate to grab each girl as she came in. Kamlesh hurried them over to Harriet and Harriet told them what to do.

They gathered in a big circle at the girls' end of the playground.

William stood by the railings and watched.

Then Wayne and Pat came along.

"Come on, man. Come and help," said Wayne.

"Yeah, it's your idea," said Pat. "You've got to help with it."

They made another circle of all the boys.

When Big Mark came zooming into the playground, everyone knew what to do.

The smallest boys and girls were safe in the middle of the circles. You couldn't expect people in the Babies' class to ignore Big Mark. After all, some of them weren't even five yet.

Everyone else began to play. They played games where you stayed together and didn't run around much.

Some of them played leapfrog. Several people had brought their Jacks, though it wasn't Jacks time.

Two girls had their skipping ropes and one group was playing Higher and Higher and another was skipping to *I saw you on Saturday night*.

In the centre of the boys' circle, a game of Thunderbirds was going strong and in the centre of the girls' they were playing *Pet Hospital*. A bossy vet was operating on a dog which had been run over. Several people told her she was doing it wrong.

Big Mark zoomed over to the boys' circle and knocked Eddie flying as he began his run-up.

Pat and William caught Eddie before he hit the ground. He grinned and winked at them and went back to leapfrog over Rav.

They all ignored Big Mark.

Big Mark revved up and br-roommed over to the girls' circle.

He banged into Carol. Carol staggered. But she went right on turning the rope. She and Georgina chanted, "L, M, N," as they turned for Jackie. Jackie

was skipping well. She said she meant to get to W before she was out. All the girls giggled and looked over at William.

Big Mark scowled. He br-roommed again, louder, and whizzed past so close that the rope nearly hit him. Jackie faltered and was out.

"Don't cry!" whispered Georgina fiercely. "Take no notice!"

Jackie gulped and went back to the end of the line.

"Well, I never got to Q before," she said. She tried to sound cheerful.

Harriet slapped her on the back.

"Well done, Jackie. And Carol," she said.

Big Mark had gone back to the boys' circle, so he didn't hear.

Then the bell went and they all lined up to go in. As they went through the door, Big Mark banged into Wayne.

Wayne hit his shoulder hard on the door jamb. He didn't make a sound. He shut his eyes for a moment. Then he went on in.

"Wayne's a great guy!" said Rav.

Chapter Seven

"It's like a strike," said Rachel, proudly.
She watched the little kids carefully,
ready to run and help them in case they
couldn't quite manage to ignore Big Mark.

Harriet nudged William. "What d'you think?" she asked. "Is it working?"

William looked all round the play-ground. They'd kept it up for two whole days now. Friday afternoon playtime was usually the noisiest but this Friday afternoon was really quiet.

"He's puzzled," he said. "I don't know. Will they be able to start again on Monday?"

"I'll tell you who's really puzzled," said Harriet, giggling. "Mrs Webber, that's who."

There was a crash. Big Mark had
banged into Rav and knocked him
against one of the big dustbins. It was
empty and the CLANGGG sounded all
over the playground.

Mrs Webber, who was on playground
duty, blew her whistle furiously and
stomped over to the
dustbins. She pulled
Rav to his feet.

"What are you playing at?" she
demanded.

Rav rubbed the back of his head and
said, "I dunno, Miss. I sort of fell."

Rachel clapped her hands, softly.

"Good old Rav!" she said.

But Mrs Webber was not satisfied. "You were pushed!" she said.

William saw Big Mark watching. He was grinning. William had to bite his tongue to stop himself telling Mrs Webber that it was Big Mark who'd pushed Rav.

"No, Miss," said Rav.

"I just tripped." He sounded surprised.

Big Mark frowned in a puzzled way. Mrs Webber frowned, too. Then she shrugged and went away to the other end of the playground where two girls were squabbling.

Rav came over to William. "That was close," he said. He grinned and poked William in the ribs. "Don't fret yourself, man, we're doing good."

Harriet and Rachel agreed. "You were great, Rav," said Harriet.

"My hero!" said Rachel.

"Aw, gerroff!" said Rav. He giggled and ran back to his game.

Kamlesh said, "William's right, though. Will everyone keep it up next week?"

They watched Big Mark. He was mooching around grumpily.
He made a sudden
grab at the
ball some
of the
smallest
children
were
playing
with.

The youngsters didn't pay any heed. They simply began to play Tig instead.

William nearly burst with pride.

Big Mark stood with the ball in his hand and his mouth hanging open.

Georgina saw and giggled. So did Carol. And Wayne. And Kamlesh and Eddie and Jackie and Pat and Rachel . . .

"Three cheers for William!" shouted someone.

"Shut up, you daft-heads!" yelled Harriet.

But it was too late. Everyone else was cheering William.

At the end of school, William went straight home. He always did, in case his mum was early. He thought he would get the letter out again and check the address once more. It made him feel closer to his mum.

As he pushed the key in the lock, he heard the garden gate click behind him. He looked over his shoulder.

It was Big Mark.

Chapter Eight

William pulled the key out again,
quietly, without unlocking the door.
He dropped it silently into
the tub of honeysuckle
beside the door. Big Mark
wasn't getting into the house!
Then he turned right round.

He didn't say anything.
He waited.

Big Mark didn't seem to know what
he wanted to do. He started to say
something and stopped. At last he said,

"It's you, isn't it? Making them all . . ."
He stopped again. He scowled at William.
William still said nothing.
Big Mark hit him.

William doubled over, clutching his ribs where Big Mark's fist had landed. He tried not to breathe for a minute. It hurt.

He squeezed up his eyes and thought of Big Mark telling everyone that William was a weed and cried when he was hit. He didn't cry.

He watched Big Mark walk back to the gate.

He watched him march away down the road. Then he left the key in the honeysuckle and followed.

He had seen something strange just before Big Mark had hit him. He had seen that Big Mark had been crying. William hadn't known Big Mark *could* cry.

Big Mark went down to the river. He mooched along, kicking stones into the water.

Presently a little girl came along, pushing a doll's buggy. The doll in it was too big for it, really, and bulged out at the sides.

The little girl stopped and fussed with her doll. Big Mark didn't stop. He was right on top of her before he even noticed her.

William yelled, "Watch it!", but it was too late. Big Mark stumbled against the buggy and knocked it forward.

It ran straight into the river.

The little girl screamed and screamed.

William ran as hard as he could to the river bank. The buggy was sliding along, not sinking much yet,  but being pulled deeper by the rush of water. William wondered if he could reach the buggy if he fished for it with a stick. He didn't think so.

"Oh, well," he said to himself, "it's a pity, but she's lost her doll and her buggy."

Then William saw a dreadful thing.

The doll moved. It wasn't a doll at all!
It was a baby – a real live baby!

Big Mark saw it at the same time.

The little girl was screaming so loudly
that William couldn't hear what Big
Mark said. He thought it was, "Go for
help!" Then Big Mark began to run
towards the road.

William looked at the river again.
The buggy was sinking, no doubt about
it. There wasn't time to wait for a
grown-up to come. The baby would be
under the water very soon.

He ran along the bank to get as near to the buggy as possible. Even in that little time, the buggy was being pulled out and out. It was in quite deep water and the baby's face was nearly covered.

William dragged his shoes off. He dived into the river, the flat racing dive

his dad had taught him, and drove himself across the current with his fastest crawl.

Chapter Nine

The soaked baby and the buggy were heavy, and William couldn't find the straps which fastened the baby in. He held the baby's head above the water and kicked as hard as he could.

The water pulled at him, and the baby screamed, and the buggy cut his hands as he fought to get the baby free from it.

He didn't feel frightened at all. He just felt furious that the buggy would not let go. He hated that buggy.

Then something gave and he felt the buggy slip down and away. It was so much easier to hold the baby up without it that William felt quite light. He was able to look around to see where they were.

They were a long way down the river and the bank wasn't near enough to reach. A man came running along the bank with a rope in his hand. He threw it to William. It fell close to him but it was no good. William couldn't catch it for he didn't dare let go of the baby for a second.

Then the man shouted "Hang on!" and pointed. There was a motorboat roaring up the river towards them.

The boat came nearer and slowed down. There was a policeman in the cockpit. He leaned out to reach William.

"Take the baby!" said William. "I'm all right."

The policeman grabbed the baby and handed it to the boatman.

Then he leaned out again and gripped William's arm. William got his other arm over the side of the boat. The policeman pulled and heaved and William rolled into the boat.

He felt terribly heavy.

Someone took his clothes off and wrapped him in a blanket. He couldn't stop shivering. That was funny, because it was a hot day.

The baby was rolled in a blanket, too. It wailed and howled and wouldn't stop.

William said, "The little girl — tell her the baby's safe."

The policeman said, "Don't worry, son. We'll look after everything."

But William was worried. "Does she know?" he asked. "She must have taken the baby out without asking. She screamed and screamed. Please tell her!"

The policeman talked on a radio. "We've been in touch with the mother," he said. "The little girl knows. Now, what about your mum, son?"

William said, "What time is it?" It seemed like hours and hours since he'd

left the front-door key in the honey-suckle and followed Big Mark.

The policeman was surprised. "It's just on five o'clock," he said.

"Oh, then she'll be at work still," said William. He remembered his letter.

"Grafton Enterprises PLC, Sixty-one Ford Street," he recited. "Mrs Waters. My name's William," he added.

"Your mate that gave the alarm told us you were William," said the police-man. He spoke on the radio again.

"Someone will go and tell your mum," he said. "We're taking you and the baby to the hospital for a check-up. Your mum will meet you there."

"I'm not ill," said William. "I'm perfectly all right!"

"Well, we'll let the doctors decide, eh?" said the policeman. "You're a very brave boy. I bet your dad's proud of you!"

William began to cry. He cried and cried. He couldn't stop, not even when the policeman carried him into the hospital and Mum was waiting there, just as the policeman had said.

Mum was crying, too. William tried hard to stop. Mum never cried.

"I'm all right, Mum,"
he said. "Why are you crying?"

"I'm crying because you're all right
and the baby's all right," said Mum.
"Isn't it silly?" She blew her nose. "What
are you crying for, William?"

"Dad," said William. He stopped
crying.

Mum said, "Oh, William, Dad would
have been so proud of you."

She hugged him again.

Then the nurse came bustling up and said William must have some tests and then he could go home.

Chapter Ten

Mum's boss, Mr Lees, was there with a car when William and his mum came

out of the hospital. Mr Lees had driven Mum to the hospital as soon as the policewoman came to the office to tell her about William.

"He was so kind," Mum told William. "I don't know what I'd have done without him."

Mr Lees shook hands with William and said, "I'm proud to know you, William."

William felt hot all over. But he liked Mr Lees. They drove home. Mr Lees wouldn't come in.

"I rang my wife from the hospital," he said. "She'll be waiting to hear all about the rescue. So will my two girls. Would you like to come over tomorrow to tea and tell them about it, William?"

William hesitated. He hadn't really told Mum yet. He wasn't sure he could tell two strange girls.

"They're both younger than you," said Mr Lees. "Look, don't come if you'd rather not."

William felt better about it. "Yes, thank you, I'll come," he said.

He hadn't visited anyone's house since Dad had died.

His mum said goodbye to Mr Lees.

William picked his key out of the honeysuckle and opened the door. His mum laughed.

"Whatever is it doing in there?" she asked.

So William told her the whole story.

She was angry when she heard what Big Mark had done. "He's being praised for raising the alarm!" she said. "And now you tell me that the whole thing was his fault! He should be punished, not praised."

"But it really was an accident," William told her. "I know it was. I saw it all. And Mark knows he knocked the buggy. I shall tell people it was an accident."

Then he said, "I couldn't have saved the baby if Dad hadn't taught me to swim and dive. I could hear him all the time, saying, 'Steady, steady does it,' just like he always did. I'm going to tell people it was my dad who really saved her."

His mum hugged him. "Do you know, William, you've never once spoken about your dad since he died? I'm so glad you can talk about him again. I've been lonely for him."

William got his name in the newspapers
and he was given a medal for saving
the baby. The baby's mother and father
gave him a huge box of chocolates and
tickets to a safari park.

William thanked them politely. He
took the chocolates to school and gave
one to everyone in his class and to all
the teachers and the dinner ladies. He
even gave one to Big Mark.

Big Mark took it. He didn't bang into
people any more. He'd told the police
that he had knocked the buggy into the
river, but when William backed him up
and insisted it really was an accident, he
wasn't a bit grateful.

"You mind your own business," he told William.

William didn't care. He was too busy talking to his friends, Rav and Harriet and Rachel and Wayne and — well everyone else in the class.

"William! Do try to scream a little softer!" said Miss Gowan.

THE END